THE NI[illegible]

Stories about Ancient Egypt

Pharaoh has ordered Dad to pick up some taxes for him - but Dad can't read. So he hires an old scribe to teach Ptoni how to understand the hieroglyphs. It's a harder job than they thought!

by Philip Wooderson

Illustrations by Andy Hammond

FRANKLIN WATTS
LONDON•SYDNEY

This edition first published in 2008 by Franklin Watts
338 Euston Road, London NW1 3BH

Franklin Watts Australia
Level 17 / 207 Kent Street, Sydney, NSW 2000

Editor: Lesley Bilton
Designer: Jason Anscomb
Consultant: Dr Anne Millard, BA Hons, Dip Ed, PhD

A CIP catalogue record for this book
is available from the British Library

ISBN 978 0 7496 8365 8

Dewey Classification 932

Printed in Great Britain

Franklin Watts is a division of Hachette Children's
Books, an Hachette Livre UK company

CONTENTS

BY ORDER OF HIS HIGHNESS, PHARAOH

ARMENLEGUP

In thanks for services rendered, the bearer of this royal scroll is granted the right to collect all taxes (now overdue) on two farms – Strong Bull Farm and Bright Star Farm, both owned by the School for Scribes at Thickutt. Run by Headmaster Blottumout.

Signed by

Chief Counsellor

DONUT

P.S. The fool who bears this is not a real Tax Collector, because he's not trained as a scribe – so he can't read this. Ha ha!

P.P.S. But don't take advantage. Or Pharaoh might get peeved!

CHAPTER 1
THE VERY BEST OMENS?

Dad was in a sunny mood, lounging in the stern of his boat, popping grapes into his mouth, as *Hefijuti* drifted down the Nile towards their destination – the school for scribes at Thickutt.

"Ah, this is the life. No more haggling. As Pharaoh's Tax Collector, I can claim ten per cent of everything they've got, lads. And they'll have to hand it over – or else."

A couple of the crew rubbed their hands. "Good for you, chief!"

"Should help you to pay our wages."

"And a little bit more would be generous, seeing as you're going to be so wealthy."

Dad was so convinced that he was going to get rich, he'd hired an old scribe to teach Ptoni how to read and write.* "So you'll grow up to be a scribe, and work for Pharaoh," Dad said. "It's the fast way to fame and fortune."

Ptoni wasn't so sure.

Stupor, the scribe, had lost all his teeth, so he lived off pots of beer. This not only made his words slurred, but fuddled his brain so much he kept drifting off to sleep.

"I'm not learning terribly fast, Dad."

Dad tilted his head. "Don't be so modest."

* You had to learn to write if you wanted a good job - see page 60

The only thing that Stupor had taught him was how to write a few numbers.

"For two potth of beer you do thith."

"For twenty potth, you do *thith*."

And Stupor had also told him you could read hieroglyphics either backwards or forwards, depending which way they were facing . . .

Dad grinned. "Keep your eyes open, Ptoni. and you might learn more at Blottumout's famous school. It's run for sons of the gentry, so there'll be lots of rich pickings."

Stupor opened one eye. "Bad omenth I thee before me."

Dad went a bit pale. "You said we'd do really well there."

"He means in the sky," said one of the lads, waving a hand at a dark cloud hanging over the desert. "We're due for a sand storm, I reckon, so it's lucky we're going ashore."

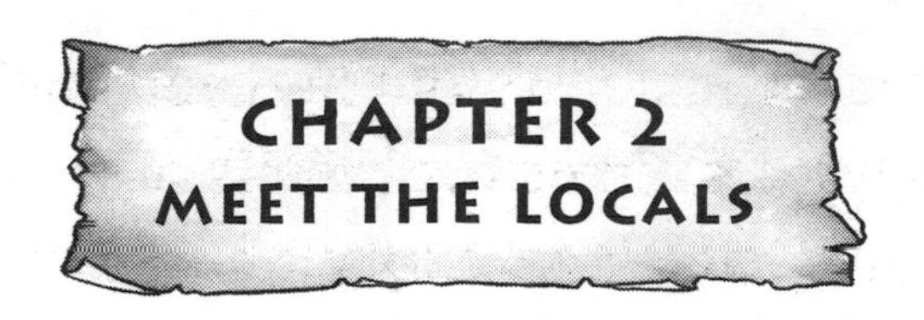

CHAPTER 2
MEET THE LOCALS

They had to share the small landing stage with another old trading boat. Two crewmen were struggling to unload a large stone sphinx in a crate, under the watchful eye of a clean little man in a white robe. He called to the lads, "Quick, quick! We need your help. This instant!"

"Excuse me?" The lads leant over the side. "Why don't *you* lend a hand?"

"I'm Skribble, Assistant Head Scribe at Master Blottumout's School."

"Big deal. We're working for Pharaoh."

"On that clapped-out old tub?" sneered the scribe, flashing his sharp ratty teeth.

"I won't have you mocking my boat. I'm a Tax Collector," said Dad.

"You couldn't *spell* Tax Collector."

Dad's ears turned brilliant purple. "Stupor," he cried, "spell Tax Collector."

No one replied.

"Never mind," Dad carried on, "where's my Royal Scroll?"

The old scribe had gone back to sleep, but Ptoni managed to find the scroll underneath some old bedding clothes. Dad hastily unrolled it to show off Pharaoh's seal.

Skribble took a step backwards.

"That's a very fine sphinx," said Dad, enjoying Skribble's confusion. "If you had ten of those sphinxes, I could take one for myself."

"Where would we put it?" asked Ptoni.

"We'd need a nice villa," said Dad. "Then it could stand by the front door and –"

"Aaaaaargh!"

CRASH!

The crewmen had been struggling to heave the sphinx out of the boat, but now it was upside down, with a bad chip on its shoulder.

"If it's too heavy," Dad offered, "I could lend you my lads in return for –"

"Dad!" Ptoni gave him a nudge.

But Skribble was now all smiles. "That silly sphinx isn't for us, sire. My goodness, we couldn't afford it. It was ordered by one of our wealthier neighbours. But may I ask what brings *you* here?"

"Your taxes, of course."

Skribble flexed his thin lips. "But the Tax Collector has been here, sire. You can't mean we have to pay twice?"

Dad flapped the scroll. "It's all down here. There's tax overdue on two farms."

Skribble sucked in his cheeks. "These two little farms had nothing to pay, so nothing can

be overdue. And we're rather busy today. We have an important guest – the High Priest from the Temple of Amun. But you can come up to the school to read through our scrolls, if you want to."

Dad looked a bit worried about this. "We'd better bring Stupor, Ptoni."

CHAPTER 3
DAD ACTS TOUGH

With Stupor wheezing behind them, Skribble led Dad and Ptoni up the dusty track, through orchards laden with fruit.

"Good harvest!" said Dad.

"Not so far," snapped Skribble.

Dad winked at Ptoni. "He's worried. Let's stay till the harvest is gathered. I bet they've got comfortable guest rooms."

"Localth!" said Stupor. "Can't stand 'em."

"What locals?"

"He must mean the boys," sniffed Skribble, as they went through the gateway. "But no local boys are allowed here. We only take the sons of the gentry. They spend their days studying scribeship."*

"Just like *my* son," said Dad.

Skribble looked slightly more hopeful. "Why don't you enrol the boy. We could give a slight discount on fees if –"

"No thanks," put in Ptoni quickly.

"My boy has his own private tutor." Dad

* You had to study for a long time – see page 61

unrolled his scroll. "Now, let's get down to business!"

Skribble skimmed a few lines, reading the last bit quite closely. He looked up and grinned. "Yes indeed. It all seems quite clear to me now. There's been a small clerical error. Some junior scribe at the palace has sent you on a fool's errand."

Dad gawped at him. "How do you mean?"

Skribble handed the scroll back. "My dear chap, before we go any further, I think I should show you something."

Leading them into the school house, he pointed at some large panels lining the walls.

"On this one, you'll see the Roll of Honour of our most illustrious pupils. At the top – Grubbiflub – now Chief Inspector of Taxes. He keeps a fond eye on his old school, and comes down very hard on any *minor* officials who think they can turn up here and stir up mischief. You'd be very silly to cross him."

Dad seemed to think for a moment. "You know, I had lunch with him once, at Merchant Kashpot's place. But he's just a *minor* official, like me, compared to the person who signed this scroll – Pharaoh's Chief Counsellor, Donut. *You'd* be very silly to cross *HIM*!"

Skribble sucked in his cheeks.

"So there!" Dad rubbed his hands. "What's on those other panels?"

Skribble shot a sharp glance at Dad. "I'm sure you can read them yourself."

"I've got a slight headache," said Dad. "Er . . . Stupor?"

Stupor lowered his beer pot.

"Forget it," Skribble said crossly. "They just list the school's main assets. A papyrus plantation and workshops to make our own scrolls.* And I have a little sideline printing the finer details onto the mummy caskets at the shrine of Anubis. But Grubbiflub taxed us

* Papyrus was made from reeds – see page 62

fairly, after taking into account the high running costs of this school."

"But not the two farms, though," Dad reminded him. "Aren't they marked on your panels?"

"Of course, yes – the one in the middle – but I told you, you're wasting your time. I mean they grow nothing at all."

"Nothing?" said Dad, with an innocent grin. "What sort of farmer grows nothing?"

"I'm a scribe, not a stupid peasant. How should I know?"

"Fine," said Dad. "In that case, why don't I see for myself?"

CHAPTER 4
VEGETABLE GARDEN?

"That's sorted *him* out," said Dad as they trudged back down the track, passing a couple of peasants picking fat bunches of grapes and putting them into big baskets. "One in ten of those baskets will soon be ours. I'm good at this, aren't I Ptoni?"

Ptoni said nothing.

Skribble had given them directions to reach the larger farm. He'd said that they should follow the posts marked with a star, turning right when they got to the fork.

"Here's the fork, Dad. You've gone right past it."

"I've got a hunch we should go left."

"But Skribble said –"

"Skribble doesn't want us to collect any taxes. Look at that great big farmhouse!"

It certainly did look smart, with pillars, palm trees, and gardens with shady bowers and statues.

"Looks like Kashpot's palace," said Dad, wiping the dust from his knees. "I could do with a mobile throne for this. First impressions count a lot when you're tax collecting. Try and act like my servants, you two."

As they approached the grand entrance, a servant girl popped her head round the doorway.

Dad said, "I'm from Chief Counsellor Donut, to take Pharaoh's dues. Fetch your master."

The girl called up the stairs. "There's some sort of dirty trader outside saying he's come from Pharaoh."

A fat man, who looked like an old bull, appeared at the top of the stairs. "Not today thank you, I'm busy."

"Taxes," Dad cried.

"What about them?"

Dad unrolled the scroll. "Read it, Stupor."

The old scribe squinted at it.

"Out loud!"

Stupor rubbed his eyes, and taking the scroll from Dad, held it an inch from his nose.

The fat man guffawed. "I know Stupor. He taught at my old school – until I fired him!"

Stupor looked up and blinked. "Oh no, Blottumout!"

“Still pretending you know how to read?”

“But *you* can’t have fired him,” said Dad.

“I happen to be the Master of this School for Scribes.”

“So you’re not a farmer?”

“A farmer? You think I’d get my hands dirty?”

“But this is your farm?” asked Ptoni.

“This is a place of retreat. For contemplation and study.”

“So who grows the grapes?” Dad burbled.

“How should I know? Why should I care? We just have a vegetable garden, providing the fare for our table.”

"Well, I shall want proof," Dad insisted.

"Not now," said Blottumout firmly.

"But I'm a Tax Collector."

Blottumout curled his lip. "And I have the Lord High Priest from the Temple of Amun coming for lunch."

"I answer only to Pharaoh. And to Donut as well," said Dad.

Blottumout wavered slightly. "Perhaps you'd like to come in and have lunch then? We have some fried fish and roast ducks."

Dad looked a bit undecided. "Tax collecting is hungry work."

“And thirthtee doo,” added Stupor.

“Palm wine,” said Blottumout, taking down a pot and pouring wine into three goblets. “And maybe you’d do me the honour of reading the text for the lecture I’m giving this afternoon. You could give us your views while we eat?”

Dad didn’t look quite so hungry. He glanced round. “Storm’s on the way . . .”

Stupor drained Dad’s goblet of wine. “And a playth of localth!”

“Shut up. We don’t want to hear about locals.”

Blottumout smiled. "Yes you will. Stupor must be referring to the other farm. It's much bigger than this and it's run by two crafty locals."

Stupor knocked back his third goblet and Blottumout quickly refilled it. "Follow the signs for the Bright Star Farm – but don't let them fool you, my friends. Don't listen, show them no mercy, and sting 'em for all they've got."

CHAPTER 5
BRIGHT STAR RICHES

Walking back to the fork in the track, Ptoni noticed that the peasants had gone, leaving their baskets of grapes.

"Thouldn't be left. Locals gettum," Stupor said to himself.

"Then we'll get 'em back," said Dad. "If Blottumout's place was the small farm, just think what the big one will be like. We'll get them to give us a slap-up lunch without any chat about lectures – then take what we want from their barns. That's Tax Collecting. I love it."

Ptoni wasn't so sure.

As they trudged round the next corner, he saw a big stone object dumped upside down in a ditch.

Dad wanted a closer look. He sank up to his knees in the water. But he didn't care. "It's the sphinx – the one we saw being unloaded."

"But why have they dumped it?" asked Ptoni.

Dad had a wild grin on his face. "Skribble was telling us the truth. Some wealthy neighbours *have* bought it – the locals at Bright Star Farm. They must have tried to hide it when they heard I was coming. Now let them try and pretend they're not rich!"

But when they got round the next bend, instead of the big swanky palace Dad was expecting to find, there was only a run-down shack.

Dad entered the dusty yard, sending two skinny geese squawking off into the bushes.

"This must be the labourers' quarters."

Lifting a sheet of stained linen, he ducked his head through the low doorway. "You peasants!" he said. "Where's the villa?"

A thin little man and his wife were squatting on the mud floor. Ptoni had seen them before. They had been picking the grapes.

"What villa?" said the wife, blankly.

"Blottumout's villa? You ought to have taken the left fork."

"We did," Dad said. "Blottumout told us that Bright Star Farm was much bigger."

"So why do we have to work on *his* land to save ourselves from starving?"

"I happen to know," said Dad, "that he's only got a vegetable garden."

"It's a very big vegetable garden."

Dad refused to be daunted. "I am entitled to take one tenth of all your produce."

"And very welcome," the woman replied. "One tenth of nothing – what's that worth?"

"Nothing?" Dad echoed.

"Afraid so."

"So what do you live on?" asked Ptoni.

The poor peasants glanced at each other.

"That's got 'em," said Dad. "What's for lunch?"

"Boiled papyrus root," said the woman. "It's in the pot on the fire."

Dad gave them a twisted grin. "I warn you, I come from Pharaoh."

"So did your colleague," she said.

"Grubbiflub," said her husband. "We were doing all right until he came and stayed in Blottumout's villa."

"What's that got to do with my lunch?"

The thin little man gave a sigh. "He wouldn't believe that we only produced enough to feed ourselves – so he took the whole lot, and our tools too."

"But how could he do that," said Ptoni. "He ought to have left you nine-tenths."

"We begged Blottumout to help us, but he said that Grubbiflub must

have worked it out because he'd consulted the panels up on the schoolhouse wall. They've been there for hundreds of years."

"That's right." Dad was nodding his head. "Those panels can't lie – so *you're* lying. If you were as poor as you claim you are, you wouldn't have bought a posh sphinx."

"We never –"

"What sphinx, your Scribeship?"

"I think they're telling the truth, Dad."

Dad looked at Ptoni in horror.

Ptoni tried to explain. "Blottumout's got the big farm. But because Grubbiflub was his former pupil, he gets away with pretending he's just got a vegetable garden. So the school doesn't have to pay any taxes. I bet you he bought the sphinx too. His garden's crowded with statues."

"Why was the sphinx brought here then?"

Ptoni tried to stay patient. "To hide it from us, of course."

Dad sighed. "So what do we do?"

Ptoni turned back to the thin man. "Have you checked what it says about this farm on the panels in the schoolhouse?"

"How could we do that? We can't read."

The woman grabbed Dad by the elbow. "Perhaps if you'd have a look, sire?"

Dad looked a bit uneasy. "I suppose I could ask my scribe here." He turned, but

Stupor was outside, slumped in the dusty yard with an empty pot in his lap.

"He might need a hand," said the woman.

CHAPTER 6
SCRIBES TELL LIES?

Stupor needed more than a hand. He had to be pushed and pulled. And halfway up the track, he turned to look back at the river. It was almost invisible now, hidden in the shadows cast by a dense dark cloud. He mumbled again. "Localth coming. Won't get any taxeth when those localth awive."

"He's mad. Ignore him," said Dad.

The schoolhouse was quiet now. There

wasn't a boy to be seen. "I don't suppose sons of gentry have afternoon lessons," said Dad, "so we can look at those panels without being spotted. That's good."

He flung open the door.

"No, it isn't."

The room was packed with boys, squatting on the floor, facing a long low platform where a frail old High Priest was stretched out on a couch, listening to Blottumout's lecture.

Blottumout stopped in mid sentence. The boys all looked round.

"Sorry," Dad said.

Blottumout beamed. "Please join us. A Tax Collector, dear boys. A shining example of what you can become if you work hard at your studies."

The boys all smirked and tittered.

Dad's legs were still splattered with mud from scrambling into the ditch. His scroll was

covered with mud too. And Stupor was just behind him, eyes shut and mouth wide open, propped up by the two poor peasants.

"To what do we owe this great pleasure?"

Dad waved a hand at the panels up above Blottumout's head. "Just need to check up on a small point."

"Indeed, reading is so important. It is sometimes necessary to check on small points. You hear that, boys?"

Dad stared at the painted panels.

"But tell us, please, why it's important."

"Important," Dad gabbled. "I'll tell you. So you won't get fooled by people – people who know how to write!"

"Only scribes can write," said the frail old priest. "And scribes are all honourable men. Why should they fool anybody?"

"Someone's fooled these poor farmers," said Ptoni.

"They're ignorant peasants," scoffed Blottumout.

"That's why they rely on scribes," said the frail priest, very calmly. "Scribes never tell lies, do they Skribble?"

"Oh certainly not. No, Your Worship."

"Our word is the Truth," agreed Blottumout, turning to gaze at the panels. "Feel free to read everything up there."

"Stupor," hissed Dad.

The farmer's wife gave Stupor a dig in the ribs. He grunted, then went back to snoring.

Dad looked even more desperate. “Ptoni?”

“I’m just starting to learn, Dad.”

“We will be patient,” said Blottumout.

Ptoni stared at the central panel. It only had a few lines of script. The symbols on the first line included one that looked like a bull. The one below showed a star. “It names the two farms.”

“Most impressive.” Blottumout turned to the boys. “Now can one of you tell me which

of the farms has the most land?"

Ptoni remembered Stupor showing him how to do numbers.

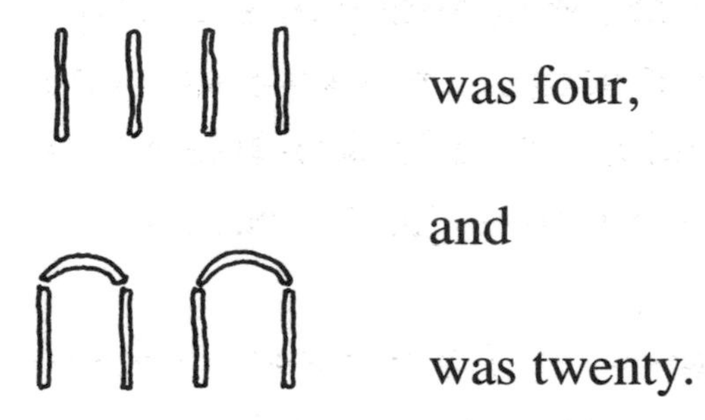

was four,

and

was twenty.

"The Bright Star Farm," they all shouted. "It's got twenty plots. It's enormous."

The poor farmers lowered their heads.

"What about Strong Bull Farm?"

"It's only got four!"

"So which farm must pay the most taxes?"

"The Bright Star Farm," they all chorused.

"Well done, boys," Blottumout beamed. "That's how the great Grubbiflub knew those two miserable peasants were farming so much land they were trying to hide their produce – because he could read hieroglyphics."

"But we've seen their farm," cried Ptoni. "They've only got two skinny geese, and four parched fields."

"Serves them right too." The High Priest wiped his hands. "Dishonesty has to be punished."

"But we never meant –" said the farmer's wife.

"Oh, quiet," said the farmer. "It's fate."

CHAPTER 7
STUPOR'S NOT STUPID

So that was that, thought Ptoni. Except that, looking up at the central panel again, he couldn't help wondering why some of the paint on those numbers looked so bright and new, and other bits looked faded and old.

"Excuse me."

"Yes," beamed Blottumout.

"Who repainted those numbers for Bright Star Farm?"

"How should I know? Some piddling junior scribe –" He turned to Skribble. "You did it."

Skribble shrank into his couch.

"What does it matter?" the priest asked.

"He made a mistake," said Ptoni.

"I don't make mistakes," cried Skribble. "I did it like Blottumout told me."

"And why would –?" Dad scratched his head. "I mean, it can't make any difference."

"It does," said Ptoni. "Can't you see – he added on new bits at the top, joining up those old uprights. That's why it looks as if Bright Star Farm has twenty plots of land."

“But if he’d done that,” said the High Priest, “both farms would be down for twenty!”

Ptoni stared at the panel again. The High Priest was right, of course, except . . . the four bold uprights marked for Strong Bull Farm did have very faint lines joining each pair of uprights, as if . . .

“Excuse me, Your Worship. Those top lines have been painted out.”

"Whatever for?" gasped the priest.

"Why do you think," Dad broke in, giving Ptoni a thump on the back. "To wangle Blottumout's villa out of paying its rightful taxes!"

Blottumout's chins started wobbling.

The High Priest struggled to sit up. "Blottumout. Quickly. Deny it!"

"I s-s-swear on my honour," he stuttered, "if I tell a lie may the gods –"

"Play some locals," said Stupor.

"Sounds reasonable," said the High Priest, raising his stick in the air. "If Blottumout lies, the god Amun will show his great displeasure by sending PLAGUES OF LOCUSTS!"*

Ptoni and Dad swopped glances.

"Is that what you meant?" Dad asked Stupor.

"What did youth ink I meant? I bin twying to tell you all day!"

They all rushed out to the courtyard.

* Locusts could do lots of damage – see page 63

The sky was black overhead. But instead of great gusts of sand, nasty black twitching things were tumbling through the air, bouncing off the ground, making a loud buzzing noise.

CHAPTER 8
HIRE-O-WHATSITS

"They'll ruin the grapes," yelled the farmer's wife.

"We'll have lost the whole crop," cried the farmer.

"It's Blottumout's loss," said Dad.

"But ten per cent would have been ours, Dad."

Dad's smile disappeared. "Not just ten per cent," he said faintly. "Blottumout tried to cheat us – and that means he tried to cheat Pharaoh – and that means he ought to be punished." His eyes went wide and glassy. "So we could claim THE WHOLE LOT!"

"The locusts have claimed the whole lot, Dad."

"So what can we take instead?"

"Phinkth," said Stupor flatly.

"Of course we're both thinking," screamed Dad.

"Not phinking. Thwinkth!" Stupor told them.

“He means that stone sphinx,” said Ptoni.

Dad swotted a big black locust off the tip of Stupor’s nose. “Do you think the lads could move it?”

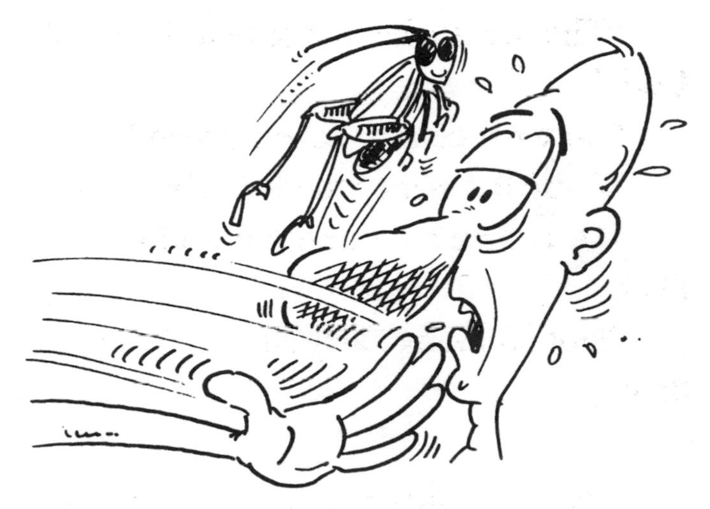

“They haven’t done anything else today.”

“Need help from the locuth!” said Stupor.

“Help from the locals?” said Ptoni.

But Dad didn’t hear. “Help from the locusts? They got us into this mess! But on the other hand,” Dad sighed, “we’d be in a far worse mess if I hadn’t had the foresight to hire a private tutor for you, to teach you those squiggly whatsits.”

"Hieroglyphs," murmured Ptoni.

"Wasted on scribes," Dad said sagely. "But don't you go scorning them, Ptoni. I think these hire-o-whatsits might turn out quite helpful for trading. We might even hire that sphinx out. For private parties."

"Thtupid!" Stupor drew himself upright. "The dwinkth will be jinkthed. I warn oo. Learning to weed ith more helpful."

Dad stared at him. "Weed? Weed what?"

Ptoni took a deep breath. "He means *read*, Dad. Like I read those Helpful Hieroglyphs!"

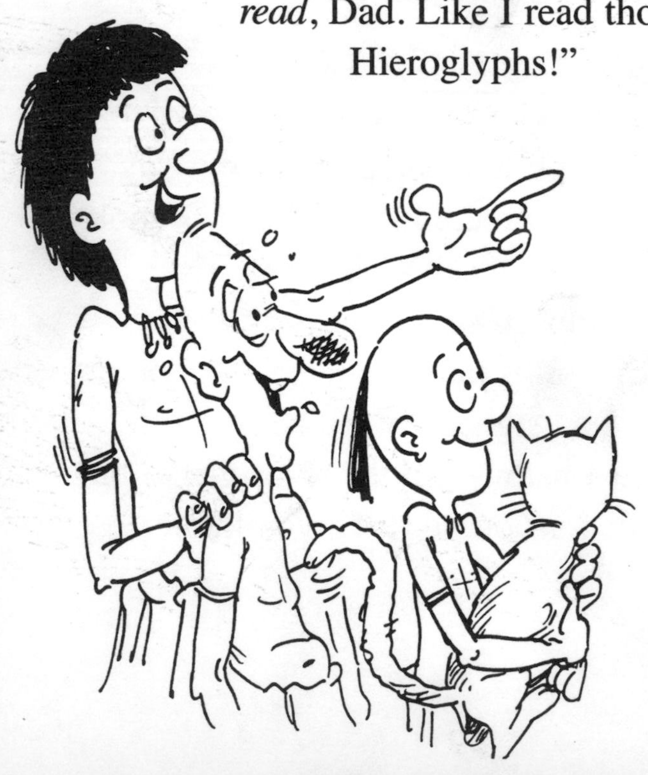

Hieroglyphics

Egyptians used a complicated writing system known as hieroglyphics. There were more than 700 different symbols to learn, and there were many different ways of writing them. Hieroglyphs could be written from left to right, right to left, or top to bottom. Very few Egyptians learnt to read and write. They relied on scribes to do it for them.

Schools for scribes

A scribe was often the son of a scribe and was taught to write by his father. But as more and more scribes were needed, special schools were set up to train them. It took four or five years for them to master hieroglyphics, but once they did, they were guaranteed a good job for life!

Papyrus

Egyptians wrote on a paper-like material called papyrus. It was made by taking the pith from riverside reeds and pounding it into smooth sheets. The papyrus was then polished, to give a smooth flat surface. To make a book, several sheets were fixed together to form a scroll, which the scribe unwound with his left hand as he wrote.

Schoolboys wrote their exercises on wooden tablets or broken bits of pottery. These materials were much cheaper than papyrus.

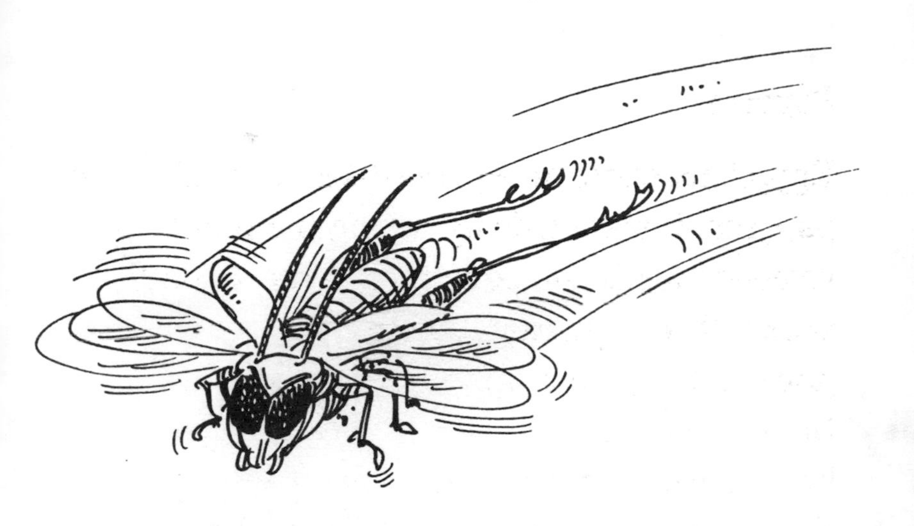

Locusts

Locusts are very large grasshoppers. They breed quickly and, when vegetation and weather conditions are suitable, they can form swarms of up to 50 billion locusts. These swarms can devastate entire crops, eating everything that grows, and bringing famine.

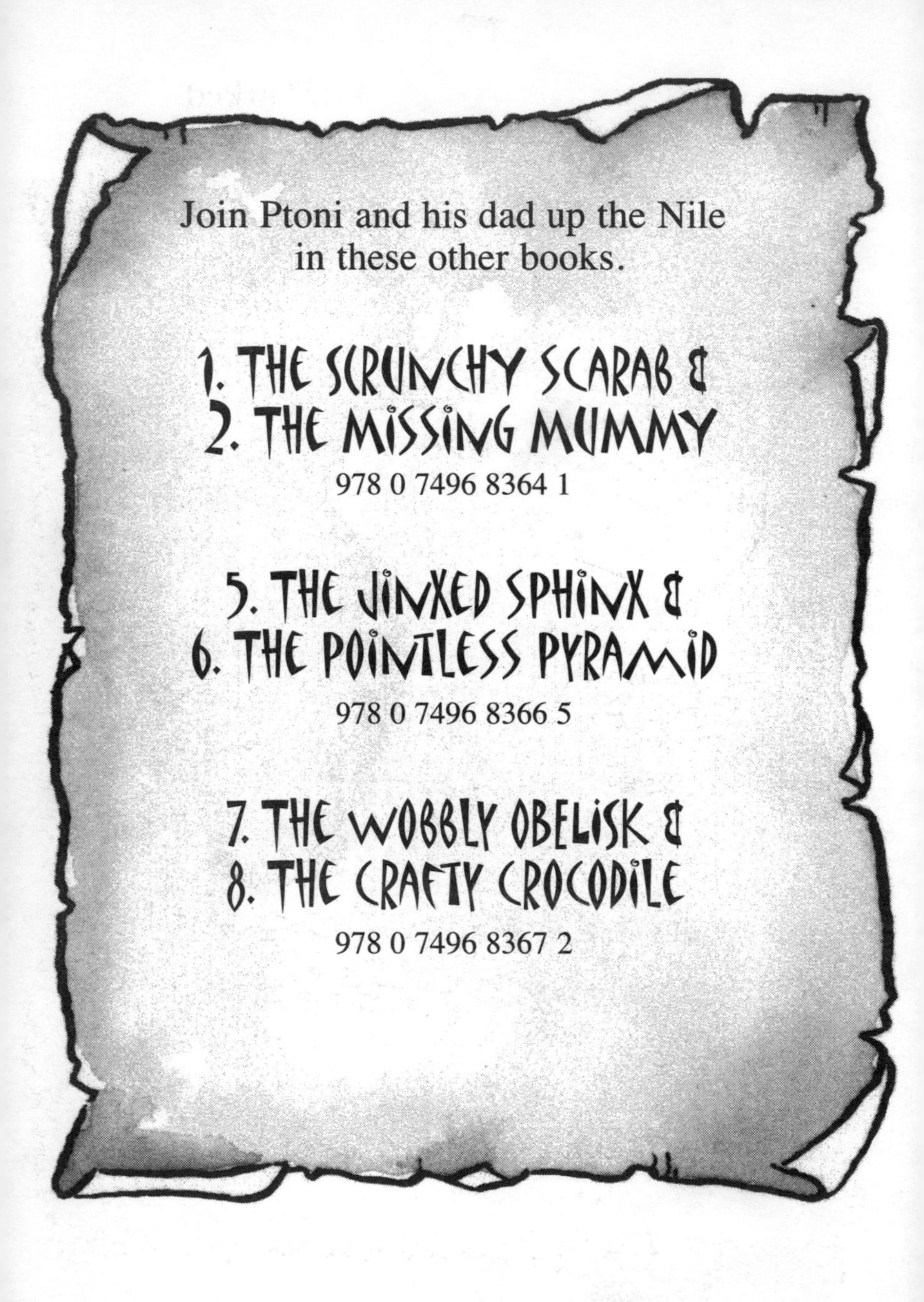

Join Ptoni and his dad up the Nile
in these other books.

1. THE SCRUNCHY SCARAB &
2. THE MISSING MUMMY
978 0 7496 8364 1

5. THE JINXED SPHINX &
6. THE POINTLESS PYRAMID
978 0 7496 8366 5

7. THE WOBBLY OBELISK &
8. THE CRAFTY CROCODILE
978 0 7496 8367 2

CONTENTS

A QUICK WORD IN YOUR EAR

After thirty years on the throne, Pharaoh Armenlegup (known as The Fearful Pharaoh) is about to celebrate the Festival of Sed.

THIS WON'T BE MUCH FUN FOR HIM.

He will have to sprint around a race course, watched by important guests who have come from far and wide. Only if he can make it to the finishing line will there be rejoicing and Good Omens for thirty more years on the throne. Then Pharaoh can put his feet up and enjoy the rest of the party.

P.S. THIS IS THE TRUTH.

CHAPTER 1
GIFTS GALORE

“Made it,” grinned Dad. “Perfect timing!”

Dad’s crew weren’t looking so happy. In front of them stretched a long line of larger boats, waiting to unload their goods at the quay.

“We’re going to be last,” said one of the lads.

“As usual.”

“No we aren’t,” said Dad, giving the

steering oar a sudden twist. *Hefijuti* cut smartly in front of a grand sleek galley, packed with soldiers wielding spears.

"Hey. Where do you think you're going?" bellowed their captain, glaring down at Dad.

"Same place as you," Dad called back. "And we've got a load of fine wines to deliver to Pharaoh – so it's urgent!"

The quay was already crowded with folk in colourful costumes and piles of sacks and boxes. There were even some big wooden cages containing exotic beasts. Ptoni counted five monkeys, a panther and one baby giraffe.

"Pharaoh buys lots of pets," said Dad, glancing at Ptiddles, the ship's cat. "Perhaps we could gain favour by throwing in –"

"No we couldn't," said Ptoni, as Ptiddles shot up the mast.

Three guards were checking through all the cargo as it was unloaded, and a scribe was scribbling notes.

"That's Anubit's last item of luggage. Now let's move on to her gifts. Three cases of prime ostrich plumes –"

"So who's this new bit then?" Dad asked the scribe.

"*Princess Anubit* is from Nubia.* She's only just disembarked. Met by the Pharaoh in person, along with his eldest son. So show some respect," said the scribe, turning back to business. "Gifts of the rarest perfumes, gold goblets encrusted with jewels, unusual Nubian wildlife –"

* Nubia was next to Egypt - see page 60

" No wine," whispered Dad to Ptoni. "Looks like we might be in luck."

"Hold on, Dad. He said *gifts*."

"*Gifts*?" Dad repeated. "Quite right. It's always best on occasions like these to give Pharaoh some small trinket." He tapped the side of his nose. "Oils the wheels of commerce. In fact, this could be our chance to get rid of that mummified cat we picked up at the shrine. We'll wrap it up so that it looks smart."

"It's already wrapped. It's a mummy. And, anyway," Ptoni stopped and looked round him, "it won't look very impressive compared with encrusted goblets and –"

"Okay, okay." Dad was unphased. "We'll just pop it in a big box and leave it on the quay."

"And hope the guards don't look inside."

"I'll make sure of that," said Dad. "You see that basket over there, between the giraffe and the monkey?"

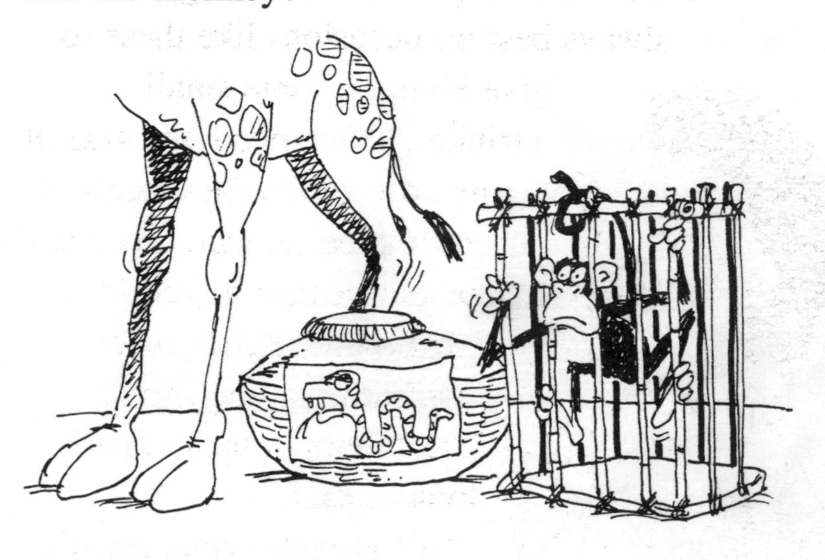

"The one with the drawing of the snake on its side?"

"Yes. What sort of fool would lift the lid and take a look in that?"

"Right, Dad, but a mummified cat's not as dangerous as a snake."

"Ptoni," said Dad, "do you really think that there's a snake in that basket? More likely

something precious, like a headdress encrusted with jewels, that the princess doesn't want stolen. So we'll draw a snake on our box too. In fact we'll go one better. We'll pop your pet snake inside."

Ptoni wavered. "Are you sure, Dad?"

"Positive. All the top traders take these safety precautions."

As Ptoni reluctantly brought out Rasp, his pet snake, he heard a great fit of squealing from one of the palace windows.

"Ooh, look at that little chap."

"He's got an enormous snake."

"What's his weedy chum up to?"

Dad raised his hand. "Dear ladies, please don't be alarmed. This snake is a pet – it's quite harmless."

He turned back to Ptoni and winked. "You know who they are? Some of Pharaoh's wives. Queen Mudpat's the one in the hat. I think I made quite an impression on them. But then, you see, I'm an expert on how to make friends at the palace."

"So what are we going to do next, Dad?"

"We'll leave our gift here, while we go and

find the Head Wine Man and give him some wine to sample. Right, Ptoni, you carry the jar."

CHAPTER 2
LOVE AT FIRST BITE

It wasn't easy to find the way – there were so many doorways and alleys. But finally they ended up in an enormous courtyard.

"The Festival site," said Dad.

On the left was a platform, shaded by canopies, with lots of colourful pennants flapping in the hot breeze. On the right were a number of booths painted with hieroglyphs. Ptoni guessed these were shrines to the gods.

"Refreshment stalls!" Dad rubbed his hands. "That's where they'll be serving our wines."

He opened the nearest doorway, but found his way blocked by a man who looked down at Ptoni's jar. "Is that the sacred oil for the shrine?" he asked politely.

"No," Dad breathed in sharply. "It's sacred *wine*. The best vintage. I can let you have thirty flasks."

The young man shook his head sadly.

"At a keen discount," Dad added. "Specially for you."

The man was wearing the finest robes and the most costly jewellery. But he was thin and pale, with eyes like muddy puddles.

"My name is Pitterpat."

"That's not your fault," said Dad, patting his back. "I once had a friend called Vomit, but that never held him back. He runs a small brewery now." Dad laughed. "You should count your blessings."

With a sorry sigh, Pitterpat told them that he'd been appointed Priest In Charge of the Festival.* "As such it is my job to make sure the Pharaoh gets round the course."

"And I'm sure you will," said Dad.

"Then I'm responsible for the celebrations."

* The Festival of Sed was very important - see page 61

"We saw all the gifts," said Dad, "and left our own magnificent offering on the quay. It'll be like a birthday party."

"Except it's a wedding," sighed Pitterpat.

"Who's getting married?" asked Dad.

"Pharaoh, of course."

"But he's married," said Ptoni, glancing at Dad. "I mean he's *very* married. How many wives has he got?"

"Twenty-nine," moaned Pitterpat. "But this

is his thirtieth year on the throne, so he wants a thirtieth bride. Urgh!"

Dad looked sympathetic. "Eaten something that disagreed with you?"

"Yes. The food of love!" Pitterpat groaned. "She's just arrived at the palace – the most beautiful girl in the world – and it was love at first sight."

"Oh dear." Dad shook his head sagely. "You're a nice enough lad, but you've got no chance against Pharaoh – besides, she's a Nubian princess!"

"But I can't live without her!"

"There are plenty more pretty young girls." Dad gave him a dig in the ribs. "Why I saw one only this morning, selling watermelons, and she –"

"OY, YOU!" a voice yelled from the courtyard. "Who do you think you're nudging?"

Ptoni turned to see three angry guards.

"He says he's called Pitterpat, poor chap," said Dad grinning at the guards. "My goodness, he's got problems."

The Head Guard drew his sword. "He's not the only one. That's *Prince* Pitterpat you're talking about. The King's-Eldest-Son-Of-His-Body-Whom-He-Dearly-Loves. And, what's more, Queen Mudpat is his mother."

Dad spun round. "The King's . . . Queen Mudpat's . . . Help!" Falling on his knees, he dragged Ptoni down beside him. "Wasn't I only just saying that this handsome young man has such a royal aura? And I wasn't nudging him. I'd spotted a small piece of dirt –"

"Who are you calling a piece of dirt?"

"Please," Prince Pitterpat turned to the guards. "This poor fellow's only been trying to cheer me up – in his own simple way. And he says he's got some fine wines to trade. Take him to meet the Head Storeman."

"It's our lucky day," Dad whispered as the guards led them through a maze of narrow alleyways. They emerged in a yard where servants were kneading bread dough, watched over by a plump little man holding a rolled-up scroll.

"What do you want?" he demanded.

"We bring some rare wines," Dad told him. "We thought, if you're the Head Storeman, you should have the honour of being the first to enjoy them."

Ptoni pulled the bung from his flask and poured some wine into a goblet provided by one of the servants.

The storeman swirled it about, took a small sip, tried to gargle, then spat it out with a cough.

Dad gave an approving nod. "The best tasters all do that, Ptoni. It keeps their palettes clear."

"Indescribable!" gasped the storeman, clutching at his throat.

"Ambrosia?" suggested Dad. "Sun-kissed peaches, perhaps, with a subtle hint of almonds?"

The storeman spat again. "I wouldn't use this in the kitchen. Not even for scouring the pots."

"Neither would I," agreed Dad. "No, this should be kept back for Pharaoh himself."

"Don't you dare to mention His Highness,"

roared the Head Guard. “You scum!”

“B-but, he’s Pitterpat’s Dad, and any friend of Pitterpat’s –”

“Don’t push it!” The Head Guard was bristling. “You’re already in big trouble for mooring your crummy boat and leaving a dangerous snake on the palace quay.”

“It’s not dangerous, and anyway it was guarding our gift for Pharaoh, a valuable sacred cat – sure to bring good luck.”

The guard gave Dad a withering glare. “And you’re going to need it, sunshine.”

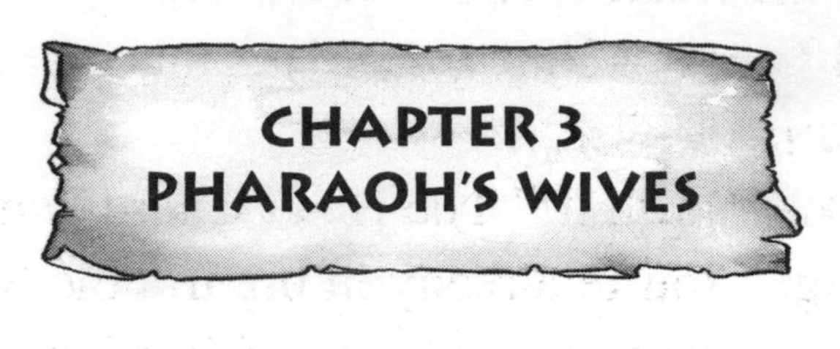

CHAPTER 3
PHARAOH'S WIVES

The guards dragged Dad across the quay.

All the barges had been unloaded and their crews were lounging on deck drinking beer. All except *Hefijuti* – its deck was still crowded with wine pots. Where were the lads, Ptoni wondered.

"Open this," said the Head Guard, whacking the box with his sword.

"It's been opened already," gasped Dad,

lifting the lid. Ptoni peered inside. Shifting a handful of straw he uncovered the cat's bandaged head.

"Ah good! Pharaoh's gift is still there," exclaimed Dad, lifting out the cat and cradling it like a baby.

"We don't want that mangy object!" The Head Guard grabbed the cat by the neck and chucked it into the river. "Hurry up! Where's the snake?"

Rasp was not in the box.

"Does Pharaoh like snakes?" Dad asked.

The Head Guard raised his sword and

looked closely at Dad. "Don't you understand, numb-skull? Snakes are strictly forbidden anywhere near the palace."

"There's another one just over there." Dad pointed across the quay.

"It's gone," Ptoni whispered. "Along with the monkeys, the panther and the baby giraffe."

"That's enough. I want this boat searched!" yelled the guard. His men rushed about, peering deep into the wine pots, and poking their spears under sacks.

"Funny things snakes," Dad murmured, fishing over the side of the boat for the mummified cat. "I mean, when you don't want to see them, they always get under your feet."

"Let's hope you find it as funny being locked up for the night." The guard turned back to Ptoni. "As for you," he scowled, "you've got until dawn tomorrow to find that snake – dead or alive. Or else your useless father is going to be buried up to his scrawny neck in sand, and left for the vultures' breakfast."

When Dad had been dragged away, protesting loudly, Ptoni sat on the deck stroking Ptiddles, who'd just scrambled down the mast.

Where could Rasp have got to?

He looked round to see the lads clambering unsteadily onto the boat.

"We've just done a deal –"

"With Pharaoh's wives –"

"Great bunch of women –"

"One of them wanted an unusual pet, so –"

"You didn't sell Rasp?" shouted Ptoni.

"Your Dad owes us six months' wages –"

"Oh, shut up!" Dodging round them, Ptoni jumped ashore. He hurried across the quay and darted through a doorway, up some stairs into the palace. Tiptoeing past a guard who was

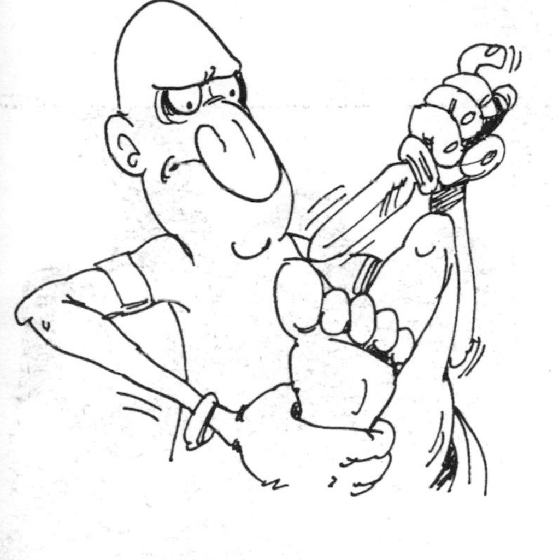

cleaning his toenails with his dagger, Ptoni went through room after room. He was following the sound of women's voices.

At last, peering round an archway, he caught sight of Pharaoh's wives. They were all squabbling and giggling until Queen Mudpat shouted. "We've now got a wonderful chance to take revenge on Pharaoh, thanks to those idiots who sold me this snake."

"B-but we might get blamed, Queen Mudpat."

"I'll make sure Anubit gets blamed. She actually brought a poisonous snake as one of her gifts to Pharaoh! Don't worry, the goddess will be on our side."

"Which one?"

"The goddess Hathor."

"But Hathor's the goddess of Love –"

"And of Beauty, Queen Mudpat."

"Exactly. She will help us get revenge on Pharaoh for scorning *our* love – and *my* beauty."

Silence.

Ptoni couldn't be sure what Queen Mudpat was plotting, but it was obvious she didn't want to be overheard. It wouldn't be wise to be caught here and taken for a spy. But as he tried

to back out, his foot caught a table leg, knocking a pottery oil lamp on to the floor.

"Who's there?"

He shrank behind the wall hanging, hoping he didn't bulge out. But then he felt something furry brushing his shin. He tried to kick Ptiddles away, but he missed. Then he heard footsteps coming up the stairs.

The guard pulled back the hanging. "OY, what have we here?"

Queen Mudpat loomed up behind the guard. She was as round as a boulder, with an angry red leathery face under her frightening headdress.

"Your Highness," blurted Ptoni, falling to his knees. "I'm sorry if I scared you. I only came to ask you if some men sold you my snake. You see, Rasp's my pet and –"

The other wives started to giggle.

"Rubbish!" snapped the Queen. "The boy's just a lying thief. Take him away. Chop his head off."

The guard dragged Ptoni downstairs. But when they got to the bottom he suddenly loosened his grip. "Right. Now listen to me. I'm going to take you to the chief. We've had a shrewd suspicion those wives were up to new tricks – and if you overheard something it

might just save your head, and spare your Dad being buried in sand . . . and earn me a bit of promotion. So everyone's happy. Let's go."

CHAPTER 4
MEET THE FEARFUL PHARAOH

The guard dragged Ptoni down a dark echoing passage, into a gloomy hall with oil lamps flickering in niches. At the far end of the chamber was a low platform with a gigantic canopied throne. Ptoni could hear puffs and grunts coming from somewhere behind it. Strange shadows loomed over the flagstones. His heart was thumping as he thought of the Fearful Pharaoh.*

* Pharaoh had the top job - see page 62

The guard pushed him forward. Screwing up his courage, Ptoni took the last few steps round the back of the throne, into the Pharaoh's presence. He stopped short in amazement. In front of him were two slaves flapping feathery fans over a thin, wizened little man who was trying to do sit-ups. A big, flabby fellow with a pasty face was holding

TWENTY SIX, TWENTY SEVEN, TWENTY EIGHT,

down his feet and counting out loud. “Come on sire, remember you’ve got to run round the course at the Festival tomorrow.”

“I’m hardly likely to forget it!” gasped the little man, fighting for his breath.

“Who’s that?” Ptoni whispered.

“That’s the Fearful Pharaoh, you fool, and his Chief Minister, Donut. Bow down,”

growled the guard. "Quick! Grovel!"

The Pharaoh sat up with a groan and a slave wiped his brow. "What have we here?"

The guard muttered something to Donut, who murmured in Pharaoh's ear. Pharaoh's left eye started twitching.

"You say you've found a spy in my wives' private quarters? How clever. How did you do that?"

"Please, Your Highness, I just went to ask your wives if they happened to have my pet sna –"

Donut's hand clamped round his mouth.

"Snail," said Donut firmly.

"You've got a pet *snail*?" asked Pharaoh. "How charming. What's he called?"

Donut removed his hand.

"Rasp, but he's not a snail. He's a –"

"SSSSSHHHH!"

Donut hissed so loudly he nearly exploded.

Pharaoh went white and his hands flew up to his cheeks. "The boy's not lost a sss . . .?"

"Snake," said Ptoni. "Yes I have. But don't worry, he's quite harmless."

"Oh–urgh! I feel faint and dizzy."

Donut glared at Ptoni.

"It's only the truth," Ptoni blurted.

"The truth?" Donut cried, pulling Ptoni into a dark corner. "The truth," he carried on in a threatening whisper, "is that Pharaoh's so fearful of you-know-whats, that the very word turns him to jelly."

It suddenly all made sense. Ptoni understood why the guards had been so worried about the snake, and why they had dragged Dad off. "We didn't know. Dad meant no harm, sire."

Pharaoh took no notice. "As if this wretched festival wasn't bad enough, without my wives having a sssecret . . ."

"Pharaoh's wives are jealous," said Donut turning back to Ptoni, "because Princess Anubit is such a gorgeous young woman. So we need to know what they're plotting."

"It's clear as day," screamed Pharaoh. "They'll let it squirm in here and –"

"Hold on, sire." Ptoni broke in, aware that this might be his only chance to save his Dad from the vultures.

"They won't let it go. They'll *keep* it."

"Whatever for?" scoffed Donut.

"To put on the course, of course. They'll hide it there tomorrow – to stop Pharaoh getting round."

There was a shocked silence.

"The lad is right," groaned Donut. "They're such

cunning devils. They'll hide it in one of the shrines that Pharaoh has to run into on his way round the course."

Pharaoh was biting his knuckles. "Oh, why did I ever agree to take on a thirtieth wife?"

"She brings great wealth," said Donut.

"And a baby giraffe," ventured Ptoni.

"It's too late to call off the wedding without great loss of face. The only thing to do is to catch the sss . . ."

"Silly thing," finished Ptoni.

Donut looked at him slightly more kindly.

"It'll soon be dark," Pharaoh snivelled.

"We could set some traps," said the guard.

"Brilliant," said Donut. "*You* can set the traps, and if you manage to catch it, I'll see you get promoted."

CHAPTER 5
SSS-SORTED?

That night Ptoni had to stay up and keep watch in Pharaoh's chamber, because Pharaoh still half-expected a snake to slip into his bed. The floor was as hard as stone and Pharaoh had noisy dreams.

"Help, there's a sss . . ."

"Mercy! Mudpat!"

Ptoni had his own wide-awake nightmares, wondering what would happen if Rasp wasn't

caught in a trap. But he must have dozed off in the end, because when he opened his eyes next, Pharaoh was doing more sit-ups and the chamber was full of sunshine.

Then the guard entered the room, bearing a basket. “I’ve got it, sire. I’ve caught your s –”

“Sssplendid,” Donut cried, letting go of the royal ankles.

Pharaoh tipped back with a thud.

“You mean I’m s-s-safe?”

“That’s right, Your Highness. You can get round the course without any fear on that subject. And I can have my promotion.”

Pharaoh stood up, looking dazed.

"No sss . . . sticking its fangs into me?"

"No danger at all," declared Donut.

Pharaoh whistled and danced a quick jig. "Tee hee!" Grabbing hold of Ptoni, he kissed him on both cheeks. "You clever boy, what can I do for *you*?"

Ptoni took a quick breath. "Could you please not bury my Dad in the sand."

"Consider it done. Set his Dad free."

As the guard hurried off to do this, there was a noisy fanfare of horns and a great procession of scribes streamed in, followed by Pitterpat.

Pharaoh greeted him brightly. "Cheer up, Eldest-Son-Of-My-Body. The sss has been sorted. Let's go!"

"We wish luck to your Highness," said Donut.

Pitterpat only managed a sigh as the procession moved off, with Pharaoh striding ahead, leaving Donut and Ptoni (and the basket containing the snake).

From the window they had a good view of the tents and the shrines in the courtyard, with the raised platform opposite, so they could watch the important guests waiting to take their seats.

Donut pointed out Princess Anubit with her retinue in bright robes gathering at one end, and twenty-nine grim-faced wives down the other end, bunched up round Queen Mudpat. But, as the horns started blaring again, Ptoni stepped back from the window to take a quick peep in the basket. He wanted to make sure Rasp was all right.

PSSSSSSSSSS!!!!!! The snake reared up.

But it wasn't harmless Rasp. This was a poisonous snake.* A deadly horned viper! One bite and you'd be lucky to live for another three minutes – never mind thirty years! Ptoni slammed the lid down. Where on earth was Rasp?

Cheering broke out from the courtyard.

"Come on, quick. It's starting," called Donut. Ptoni rushed back to the window.

Pharaoh leapt the first two hurdles and bounded towards the first booth like a young antelope.

"Shrine of Isis," Donut shouted into a cone-shaped tube that amplified his voice over the heads of the crowd. "God of Death and Rebirth." Then he turned and whispered to Ptoni. "That's the place where the guard trapped your snake. Lucky for your Dad, though not for the buzzards. Tee hee!"

* Egyptian snakes could be highly dangerous - see page 63

Ptoni didn't think it was funny. Rasp was still out there somewhere. His eye was caught by Mudpat, straining forward as Pharaoh came sprinting out. Her gaze didn't flinch. She was waiting – waiting for something to happen.

Then Ptoni saw Princess Anubit tugging her chunky earrings and looking across at Pitterpat. He remembered Mudpat saying that a dangerous snake had been one of her gifts. Perhaps Anubit had hidden it in the sacred booth, hoping it would bite Pharaoh because she couldn't bear the thought of marrying such an old man? But it had been caught in the trap that had been meant for Rasp.

"Great Pharaoh takes the last lap easily in his stride," Donut declared to the crowd as

Pharaoh lurched over a hurdle, knocking it hard with his shin.

He didn't look quite so perky now, with sweat dribbling down his cheeks and veins pulsing all over his forehead. He was fighting for breath. He was gasping. He nearly tripped up, but he staggered on – into the final booth.

"The shrine of Hathor," boomed Donut. "Goddess of Love and Beauty!"

Ptoni winced. Mudpat sucked her cheeks in. The other wives all leant forward.

Then there was a terrible scream.

"YAAAAAAAAAAAAA!"

"And he's out!" cried Donut.

CHAPTER 6
SSS-SPECIAL EFFECTS

Mudpat jumped to her feet, knocking off her headdress, but that didn't stop her from grinning. As for all the junior wives, they were flapping about like small birds, twittering with excitement. Even Pitterpat managed a smile, though it was soon wiped from his face as Pharaoh bolted at top speed across the finishing line. The crowd erupted with wild cheers.

"Yes, Pharaoh has made it," boomed Donut. "And what an amazing last spurt. Good Omens for thirty more years of Pharaoh's Glorious Reign."

Pharaoh collapsed in the dust. He lay there panting for breath, gasping out "Sssssend that boy to me!"

Donut's hand fell on Ptoni's shoulder. "He's thinking of you. What an honour."

As he was led through the crowd, Ptoni only expected the honour of being buried in sand next to Dad. Though Dad didn't look too

worried. Ptoni could see him helping to lift Pharaoh onto a couch. Slaves gathered round with towels, ready to rub him down, while

others started to fan him with plumes of ostrich feathers.

Then Donut was booming again. "Now the gods have shown their pleasure in Pharaoh's great fitness and health, I am proud to announce Pharaoh's plans for a Royal Wedding!"

Mudpat and the wives did not look very pleased.

Prince Pitterpat looked even less pleased. Princess Anubit looked *desperate*.

And then Ptoni saw two guards lugging another basket out of the shrine of Hathor.

Pharaoh pointed a shaky finger. "Do you know what's inside that basket? It nearly scared me to death."

"But my pet helped you to finish," cried Ptoni.

"Your pet?" Pharaoh croaked. "But if that's yours, where did the other one come from?"

"It was her gift," bellowed Mudpat waving a fist at Anubit. "I'd chop off her head!"

Pharaoh darted a glance at the unhappy princess, before looking back at Queen Mudpat and his other twenty-eight wives.

"You monsters don't want me to marry again, but neither does my bride to be. Or not to be. That is the question." He wiped his brow. He was trembling. "But if I back out now, everyone will titter. Oh, what am I going to do?"

Ptoni screwed up his face, trying his best to look puzzled, but there was an easy answer. "Please sire, excuse me saying, but why don't you ask Pitterpat . . ."

"Ask him what?"

Ptoni took a deep breath. "If he'd marry her for you."

Pharaoh blinked. "For me, you mean? Just to help his old Dad?"

"He'll do as he's told," said Donut. "I mean, Pitterpat's very loyal."

"Loyal to ME," Mudpat cried out. "He's my eldest son as well and he'll do whatever I tell him!"

"How helpful," murmured Pharaoh, wiping more sweat from his brow.

Donut cleared his throat. "So as I was saying, I'm proud to announce Pharaoh's plan for the beautiful Princess Anubit to wed Prince Pitterpat, the King's-Eldest-Son-Of-His-Body-Whom-He-Loves-More-Dearly-Than-Ever!"

Mudpat sat down with a grunt. Pitterpat gawped at the princess, a huge smile spread across her face. And then he was running towards her. And soon they were hugging and

kissing. And everyone else was cheering, "Great Pharaoh is fearful, but wise, too!" and Pharaoh was blushing. "It'sssss nothing."

CHAPTER 6
DAD GETS HIS DUES

The wedding took place on the next day.

Ptoni and Dad were asked to the banquet. They sat at the lowliest table, but in the middle of the feast Donut came down to join them.

"A message from Pharaoh," he murmured. "As a small token of his thanks for things turning out so well, he commands you to collect and transport to him the taxes due from two of his Royal farms."

Dad frowned "Is he going to pay us to do that?"

Donut winced. "The dues should be worth a small fortune, dimwit, and you'll get ten percent of them."

Dad threw a quick glance at Ptoni. "Ah well," he suddenly grinned, "in that case the answer is yes. I knew we'd do well at the palace. Didn't I tell you, Ptoni?"

"Yes, Dad."

"When you know the ropes as well as I do, Ptoni, there's nothing to be afraid of. Not even a Fearful Pharaoh!"

NUBIA

The country of Nubia lay to the south of Egypt, and it was ruled by Egypt for many centuries. Nubians were great traders selling ostriches, apes, leopard skins, giraffes' tails, ebony and ivory.

THE FESTIVAL OF SED

The Festival of Sed happened after a Pharaoh had reigned for thirty years. It showed that he was still fit to wear the crown and confirmed his right to rule. Spectators from all over the country gathered at the palace and cheered as the Pharaoh ran round a special course. When he succeeded (as he always did) then he was recrowned. The celebrations lasted for weeks and the whole country came to a standstill.

PHARAOHS

The Egyptians called their kings "Pharaohs". The word means "the Great House" in Egyptian and referred to the palace. The position of Pharaoh was inherited, and passed to the eldest son of the Pharaoh's chief wife.

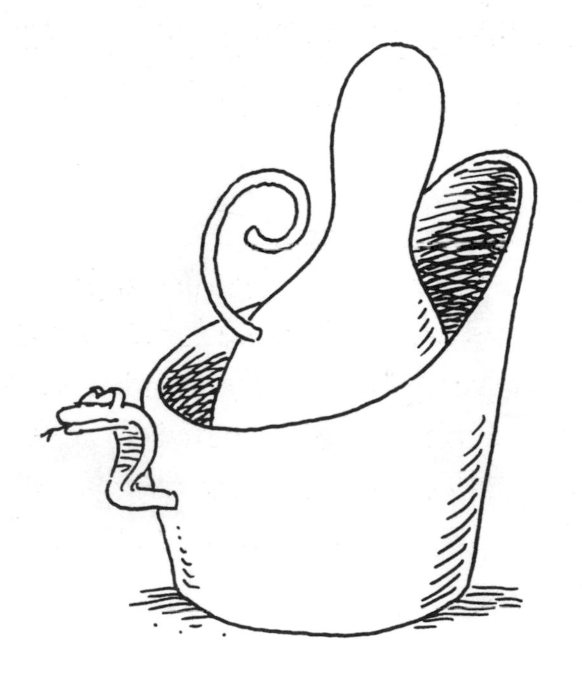

SNAKES

Work in the fields meant Egyptians might be bitten by several kinds of snake. The sand and horned vipers were particularly dreaded. Death followed a few minutes after their bite. The cobra was regarded as a particularly powerful snake, and a replica of one adorned all the Pharaoh's crowns.

Now turn this book around to read

THE HELPFUL HIEROGLYPH